THIS BOOK BELONGS TO

The Christmas Bear

The Christmas Bear

By Henrietta Stickland Illustrated by Paul Stickland

RAGGED BEARS

Little Bear lived at the top of the world.

One Christmas Eve night, he left his parents in their snuggly den to explore. Little Bear followed his nose. It led him over the hill to a big, bright hole in the snow. I wonder who lives down there? thought Little Bear.

He followed his nose further and further into the hole until all of a sudden . . .

Little Bear fell in!

Down . . . down . . .

down he fell . . .

. . . until he landed with a *bump*! at the bottom.

'Little Bear!' said a friendly voice. 'What a tumble!'

Little Bear peeped between his paws and saw a jolly man smiling down at him.

'I'm Father Christmas,' said Father Christmas. 'How kind of you to drop in. I could do with some help.'

'Letters, letters, letters!' said Father Christmas as he showed Little Bear the Sorting Room. 'So many children, so many presents!'

Little Bear helped sort some letters. But there was so much to look at – and where was that penguin going? he wondered.

'**M**y Workshop!' said Father Christmas proudly as he
hurried Little Bear into the next room. 'We make all the toys
here – teddies, trains, dinosaurs . . . you name it.
I've designed one or two myself,' admitted Father Christmas
with a chuckle.

Little Bear wanted to make some toys, too, but there was
so much else to see.

Next Father Christmas took Little Bear into a room full of noisy machinery.

'This is the North Pole,' he shouted. 'We use it to make our own electricity. It's quite simple.'

Little Bear nodded his head as if he understood, but really he didn't and he was watching the naughty penguin.

'**H**ere's a lovely job for you,' said Father Christmas, as they arrived in yet another room. 'Testing all the toys!'

Little Bear was so excited, he couldn't think where to start.

'**T**esting, testing!' said Little Bear as he squeezed a teddy's tummy.

'*Grrr*!' growled the teddy.

'You'll do,' said Little Bear. 'Now where's that penguin?'

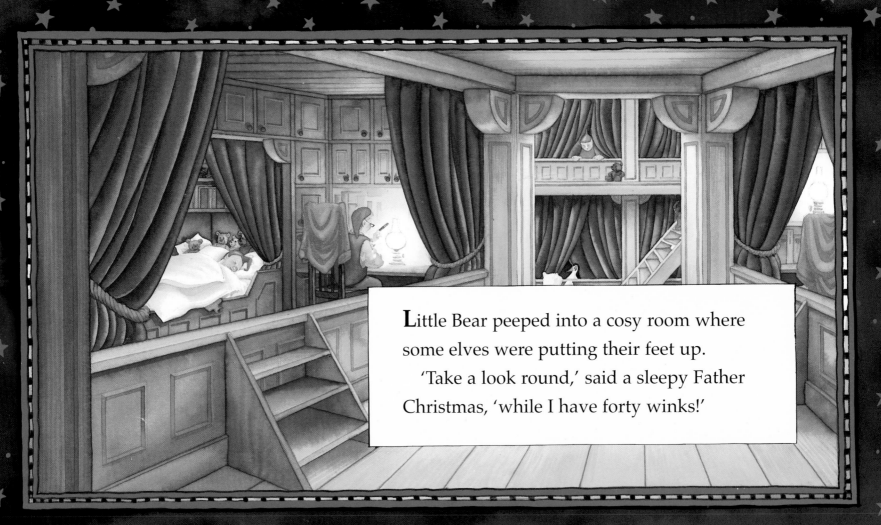

Little Bear peeped into a cosy room where some elves were putting their feet up.

'Take a look round,' said a sleepy Father Christmas, 'while I have forty winks!'

Little Bear followed his nose to the kitchen. There was a delicious smell of baking. Soon it was time for tea. Little Bear sniffed.

'Fish and ice cream,' he said. '*Grrreat!*'

'**B**ack to work again,' exclaimed Father Christmas, taking Little Bear into the storeroom. There were lists to be checked and toys to be found for children all over the world. It kept Little Bear busy for hours.

I wonder if there's a present for me? he thought, shyly.

'This is the Present Wrapping Department,' Father Christmas informed Little Bear when they got there.

Little Bear had never seen so many presents and so much wrapping paper.

'Not long now,' said Father Christmas. 'Look. There goes a sack of toys down to my sleigh.'

Father Christmas and Little Bear went to the stable.

'Nearly time to go,' said Father Christmas to his reindeer. 'And more cats to feed, I see.'

'Mice, too,' said Little Bear.

'Well, Happy Christmas, cats and mice,' said Father Christmas. 'Now we must be off!'

Father Christmas reached into a pile of presents and gave one to Little Bear. 'This one is for you,' he said with a smile. 'My Little *Christmas* Bear.'

'Oh, thank you!' cried Little Bear.

'I… er, made it myself,' said Father Christmas. 'I think it's rather special. Now, climb in, Little Bear.'

'First stop, the top of the world!' said Father Christmas,
and in a wink they were safely back at Little Bear's home.
   'Open your present, Little Bear,' said Father Christmas.
   'It's a book, and it's all about ME!' said Little Bear.
   'Time I was on my way,' said Father Christmas.

'Goodnight, Little Bear!
And a very Merry
Christmas to you all!'

For my grampa, artist and illustrator
Geoffrey Squire
P.S.

For Emily, Little Etta, Katie, Danda, Erica,
Thomas, Katharine and Charlie, with much love
H.S.

This edition published in the UK in 2006 by Ragged Bears Publishing Limited,
Milborne Wick, Sherborne, Dorset DT9 4PW.
www.raggedbears.co.uk

First published in UK in 1993 by Orion Children's Books

Distributed by Airlift Book Company, 8 the Arena, Mollison Avenue,
Enfield, Middlesex EN3 7NL. Tel: 020 8804 0400.

A CIP record of this book is available from the British Library

ISBN HB 1 85714 365 5
PB 1 85714 366 3

Printed in China

A selection of books by Paul Stickland published by Ragged Bears

Truck Jam

Trucks rumble and roll in this big chunky pop-up book of vehicles. With seven generous sized double spreads of pop-ups, young truck fans will be kept amazed and amused even stuck in traffic!

£11.50 • PS88 • ISBN: 1 85714 158 X

Big Dig

A fantastic pop-up book with all the machines you would expect to see on a building site – a bulldozer, an excavator, a giant crane - and much, much more! The ideal book for any child who is obsessed with big machines.

£12.99 • PS86 • ISBN: 1 85714 249 7

Monkey Business

A gloriously ebullient pop-up book that explores the world of the jungle. As the monkeys invite the other animals to visit the new babies in their 'family tree', three-dimensional tigers and alligators jump towards the reader, elephants swing their trunks and giraffes reach up high above the forest. A must for all animal-mad children.

£12.99 • PS225 • ISBN: 1 85714 274 8

Dinosaur Roar!

Dinosaurs of every size, shape, colour and personality thunder through the pages of this fun-filled book of opposites. The infectious rhythm of the bold rhyming text will have every child ROARING for more!

Paperback • £4.99 • PS04 • ISBN: 1 85714 293 4

Dinosaurs Galore!

A monster pop-up celebration of *Dinosaur Roar!* A wonderful interactive pop-up book – see all your favourite dinosaur images POP into life!

£12.99 • PS85 • ISBN: 1 85714 277 2

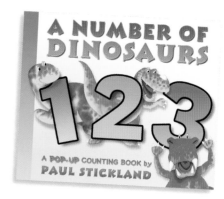

A Number of Dinosaurs

One little dinosaur, add one more, makes two little dinosaurs! The pop-up numbers in this brilliantly inventive counting book get bigger and bigger and better and better as they grow from 1 to 10. Learning numbers has never been so much fun!

£10.99 • PS82 • ISBN: 1 85714 364 7

Visit our website **www.raggedbears.co.uk** for a full list of all our products to buy plus lots of fun and games and free downloadable activities to enjoy.